*To my mum Pat, who encouraged me to do my homework in between kicking a ball all around the house, and is still with me every step of the way.*

# FRANKIE'S
# MAGIC
# FOOTBALL

# BY FRANK LAMPARD

# CHAPTER 1

Frankie ran out on to the school field in his PE kit, excited about another game of football. The other kids were already doing stretches, and Charlie had his goalie gloves on. Charlie *always* had his gloves on. He never knew when he might be called on to save a goal. Louise was doing keep-me-ups. As Frankie approached, she turned and blasted a low curling shot at Charlie. He was still stretching, but dropped to his right and snatched up the ball.

"Always ready!" he said. "You won't catch me out."

He tossed the ball back, but a hand caught it in the air. It was Mr Donald, their PE teacher. He was carrying a sack, and kicked the football back towards the sidelines. "Won't be needing that today," he said.

"What?" gasped Frankie. "How are we going to play football without a football?"

"Donaldo's gone nuts," muttered Charlie.

"I heard that!" said their teacher, with a smile. "We're going to do something a little different." He turned the sack upside down and out fell a long wooden bat, a small ball, a glove and some plastic cones.

"Baseball!" said Louise.

"That's right, Louise," said Mr Donald. "Football isn't the only sport in the world."

Frankie knew he was right, but he was still a bit disappointed.

Mr Donald began to lay out the cones in a diamond shape around the field. "Baseball is all about tactics, hand—eye coordination and running," he said. "It might help your football game in ways you don't realise. In the United States, baseball is the national game, just like football is here."

"Can't hurt to try," said Louise, looking at the others.

Frankie shrugged. "Why not?" he agreed.

Five minutes later, Frankie stood with his feet planted on a batting plate, holding the baseball bat in his hands. Charlie crouched behind him, wearing a mitt.

"I'll bowl!" said Louise.

"It's called 'pitching'," Mr Donald explained, throwing her the baseball. "Right class, the rules are very straightforward – the batter gets three chances to hit the ball. If he misses and Charlie catches it, it's called a 'strike'. Three strikes and you're out. Understand?"

They all nodded. Frankie thought he was keeping up.

"Good. The other way you can be out is if you try to run to one of the bases and someone gets there before you with the ball." Their teacher took a big breath. "Or you can be caught out."

Charlie whispered to Frankie,

"About the same number of rules as football, then."

The rest of the class were either fielding, which meant standing around in the field waiting to catch the ball if Frankie hit it, or lined up ready to bat.

"Ready?" said Louise.

Frankie nodded, hands tightening on the bat.

Louise drew back her arm, then hurled the baseball. It flew so fast that Frankie hardly saw it. He swung the bat, but heard a *thud* behind him. He turned and saw the ball in Charlie's mitt. How did that happen?

"Strike one!" called Mr Donald. "Great pitch, Louise."

She grinned as Charlie threw the ball back to her.

"Watch the ball, Frankie," said Mr Donald.

Frankie took a deep breath, lifting the bat again. *I'll be quicker this time*, he promised himself.

Louise tossed the ball from hand to hand, then pitched again. The ball seemed to curve in the air. Frankie swung with all his strength, spinning off-balance.

*Thud.*

"Strike two!"

Frankie couldn't believe it.

"One more and you're walking," said Mr Donald in a bad American accent.

Louise caught the ball, narrowing her eyes. *She's good at this!* thought Frankie.

He hoisted the bat over his shoulder, letting his knees bend a little to keep his body stable. Louise pitched once more. Frankie kept his eyes on the ball the whole way.

*CRACK!*

He felt the contact through his hands, arms and shoulders, and watched the ball shoot high over Louise and Mr Donald. It flew right

to the back of the school field,
landing in a bush.

"Home run!" cried Mr Donald.

"That was more fun than I
expected," said Frankie, as he,
Louise and Charlie walked home
from school. They were heading to
the park for a quick kick-around.
No day was complete without a
game of football!

"You were a natural," said Louise.

Frankie blushed. He'd scored three
home runs in the end. "You were
both pretty good too," he said to
his friends. Charlie hadn't missed a
single catch, and Louise had earned

more strikes than any other pitcher.

As they entered the park gates, Frankie noticed something very strange. "Charlie – you're not wearing your gloves!"

Charlie smiled. "It's okay – I'll put them on in a minute."

But when he looked in his bag, Charlie went pale. He pulled out one of his gloves, and a baseball mitt.

"Oh no!" he said. "I must have got them mixed up after PE."

"It's okay," said Louise. "You can get the other one back tomorrow. Why not just use the baseball one for now?"

"I guess so," said Charlie, slipping them both on. He didn't look happy.

Charlie took his place in the goal and Frankie tipped his magic football out of his bag. Only it hadn't been all that magic recently. They'd played with it a few times, and nothing had happened. *Perhaps the magic has run out?* Frankie's heart sank at the thought that they wouldn't have any more adventures, but at least they'd had plenty of fun.

He kicked the ball to Louise. She let it run to her right foot, then booted it towards the top corner of

Charlie's goal. Frankie thought his friend had no chance, but Charlie leapt up, stretching out his baseball mitt. At the moment the football hit the leather, it vanished.

Frankie blinked. "Where's it gone?"

He felt a tingle down his spine, as the glove on Charlie's hand started to glow. "It's getting warm!" his friend called over.

Frankie and Louise ran to his side as strange tendrils of sparkling light spread from the mitt, wrapping around each of them. Frankie let the coils of light encircle him. He began to feel light, as if he was being lifted off the ground.

Then, with a sharp tugging sensation, the park disappeared before his eyes.

## CHAPTER 2

Frankie could hear a woman's voice.

"The statue itself is 46 metres high. She was designed and built in France, but then shipped over to America in pieces."

*What's she talking about?* wondered Frankie.

Slowly the scene around him

swam into focus. He was standing at the back of a group of people all taking pictures with cameras. The voice belonged to a woman in a uniform. Her name tag read: *Dana DuPont, Official Guide*. They were standing in a room, with strange-shaped windows. Through the glass, Frankie saw stretches of blue sky and tall buildings. *Really* tall buildings.

"Where are we?" whispered a voice near his feet. Frankie looked down and saw his dog, Max. One of the best things about the ball's magic was that it brought the whole team together and they were able to hear Max speak.

"It took six months to erect the statue," the woman in the uniform continued, "and work was completed in October 1886."

Louise walked over to a window, pointing at the sky. Above them, Frankie saw an enormous green arm holding up a sculpted torch. "Recognise that?" she said, beaming. She turned to Frankie and the others. "We're in the Statue of Liberty!"

"No kidding," said one of the tourists.

Everyone laughed, and Louise blushed. Frankie and Charlie joined her. "Wow!" said Charlie.

Frankie was speechless. In the distance, over a patch of water, he could see what looked like an island covered in incredibly tall skyscrapers, bristling like needles into the sky. "It can't be . . ." he muttered, as the truth hit him. "We're in New York City!"

"And that's Manhattan, I think," said Louise.

"Will someone give me a leg up?" grumbled Max. "All I can see are people's feet."

Frankie lifted his little dog to the edge. Max whined a little. "Okay, that's quite high enough. Put me down before I'm sick."

The guide was continuing to talk about the statue.

"The glove has brought us to America!" whispered Louise.

The guide started moving towards a set of stairs. "Right folks, if you'd like to follow me back down, that's it for the tour."

The tourists tramped out, but Frankie and his friends stayed behind. He could hardly take his eyes off the view. The soaring buildings seemed squeezed so close together. He realised they must be standing right at the top of the statue's head, in the crown.

"I've always wanted to come to New York," said Louise. "Times Square, the museums, Broadway, Central Park . . . "

"Hot dogs," said Max, licking his lips. "Real, American hot dogs . . . "

"The question is — *why* are we here?" said Frankie.

Charlie gripped the edge of the viewing platform. "Uh-oh," he said. "Looks like the boat's leaving."

Tourists were filing on to a ferry at the water's edge below. That was the only way back to the main island. "Quick — let's go!" Frankie said.

They ran for the stairs and

scampered down. And down . . .

. . . and down . . .

. . . and down . . .

Frankie wasn't sure how many steps there were — well over three hundred, he reckoned. When they reached the bottom, they emerged on to a path that cut through grassy parkland. The boat was already chugging across the water back towards the city, trailing white water in its wake.

"Hey!" Frankie called. "Come back! We're still here!"

He watched the boat shrink into the distance.

"It's okay," said Charlie in a shaky

voice. "We can just wait for the next one."

"Hmm . . . not sure about that," said Louise. She was standing next to a noticeboard with a clock. "That was the last boat of the day."

Frankie stared up at the gigantic statue on its pedestal, then around at the empty paths. "I guess we're stuck here for the night," he said.

"Seems like it," said Louise. She shivered. "It's cold too – we need to find somewhere out of this wind."

They walked back towards the statue's base. Perhaps they could shelter inside.

"I'm hungry," Max grumbled. "I'd kill for a bone right now."

Frankie didn't know what to say. Normally, the magic football sent them on some sort of mission. But with no one about, what were they supposed to do?

As they rounded one of the corners at the bottom of the statue's base, Frankie heard a noise. It was a rhythmic knocking sound every few seconds.

*Perhaps we aren't on our own . . .*

Max lowered his nose to the ground and scampered away. Frankie and the others went after him.

At another corner, Max stopped and pricked his ears. Frankie peered around and saw what was making the noise. A boy was tossing a baseball repeatedly against a wall and catching it on the rebound. His shoulders were sagging.

As Frankie stepped closer for a better look, his foot scuffed the ground. The boy's head jerked around.

"Hey! Who are you?" he said, his eyes wide.

Frankie came out from his hiding place. "Don't worry — we're just . . . lost, that's all. I'm Frankie."

"Hi," said Louise as she stepped

out too. Charlie and Max followed. "These are my friends," said Frankie. "Louise, Charlie . . . and Max, my dog." Max had started nosing around a bin.

The boy frowned. "*Lost*? You sure are! You're not supposed to be here."

"So how come *you're* here?" said Charlie.

The boy slipped the baseball in his pocket. "My dad looks after Ellis Island, on the night shift. My mom works late shifts too, at the hospital, so I'm stuck here. I'd better get my pa — you've missed the last boat back to the mainland."

As the boy began to turn and walk away, Max whined from the bin. "I can smell hot dog in here . . ." he said.

"Max, quiet!" said Frankie.

The boy paused and frowned at Max. "Okay, what's going on here?"

"You wouldn't believe it," said Frankie.

"Try me," said the boy. "And my name's Ernie, by the way."

Frankie glanced at his friends. Louise shrugged.

So Frankie explained, as briefly as he could, about the magic football, and how it had brought them to the top of the Statue of Liberty.

Ernie grinned. "You people are crazy," he said. "You're right, I don't believe you. Why would your magic football bring you here?"

Frankie shrugged. "Normally we have to fix something, or help someone."

Ernie smiled, a little sadly. "Well, I wish you could help me," he said. "Today's the try-out for the Yankees' junior team, and I'm stuck here."

"The baseball team?" said Frankie.

"Yeah," said Ernie. "It's my dream

to play pro-baseball one day. But I can't go, because both my folks are working."

Frankie turned to his friends. "That *must* be why we're here!" he said. "To get Ernie to his try-out!"

Ernie laughed. "Thanks, Frankie, but the try-out has already started, up at the Yankee Stadium in the Bronx. Even if there was another boat, we'd need the fastest cab in the world to get there before it finishes."

Louise's eyes gleamed. "Or a magic football," she said.

Ernie rolled his eyes. "So where is this so-called magic soccer ball?"

"I . . . I don't know," said Frankie. "The last time I saw . . . "

A tremendous creaking sound made everyone look up. Frankie's mouth went dry. The arm of the Statue of Liberty was moving! Charlie staggered into Louise, who tripped over Max.

"It's falling over!" cried Ernie, cowering beside them. "Look out!"

But it wasn't falling. The statue's enormous foot flexed and stepped off the pedestal, crunching on to the ground a few metres away. She lowered her hand, and her fingers unfurled into the water, her huge shadow falling over Frankie and his friends. The statue scooped something from the sea, and water poured between her fingers. She turned towards them. Her lips moved and there was a sound like rocks grinding.

"Looking for this?" she said.

In her hand was the magic football.

# CHAPTER 3

Frankie gaped. The hairs on his neck stood on end. The others were speechless as well.

"Does this belong to you?" asked the statue. Her breath blasted over them like a gale, whipping Louise's hair.

"Y . . . Y . . . yes," said Frankie.

The statue gently placed the ball by Frankie's feet.

"I didn't realise the Statue of Liberty moved," said Charlie.

"It's not in the guide books," said Louise.

"This can't be happening," said Ernie. "Am I dreaming?"

"Did I hear that someone needs some help?" said the statue, with a smile.

Louise pointed to Ernie. "He has to get to the Yankee Stadium. It's the chance of a lifetime."

The statue turned her head slowly towards the skyscrapers in the distance, looking across the water. Then she extended her hand towards them. Her fingers were like tree trunks.

Frankie looked at Ernie. "I think she wants us to climb on!"

A slow smile spread over Ernie's face. "I'm not going to refuse the Statue of Liberty. Are you?"

Frankie went first, stepping up and edging along the statue's finger, before settling in her palm.

"Ooh, that tickles!" she said.

Ernie came next, and the others followed. "I'm not sure how I'll explain this to my dad," said Ernie.

"Ready?" asked the statue.

"I think so," said Frankie.

The statue cupped her hand and rose to standing again. Frankie clung to his friends as the ground shot away beneath them. In just a second, they were a hundred metres up.

Max had clamped his eyes closed and was whimpering.

"Is your dog all right?" said Ernie.

"He's scared of heights," said Charlie.

"I'm scared of *falling*," said Max.

"I guess a talking dog doesn't seem that weird any more," said Ernie.

Gazing between the statue's fingers, Frankie saw her lift a

foot and step out into the water,
throwing up a huge wave. Her leg
sank beneath the surface up to the
knee and her whole body juddered.
Then she stepped with her other
leg, right off the island and into the
sea. With lumbering strides, she
surged through the water.

"How deep is it here?" said Louise, gripping one of the fingers.

"I guess we're about to find out," said Charlie.

With each stride, the water lapped higher up the statue's body. Had she done this before? Did she even know if she could get to the other side? The water reached her waist and kept rising. Then it was over her chest. Frankie looked at the looming skyscrapers ahead, then back at the island where they'd come from, with its empty pedestal. *We're not even halfway!*

The water churned around the statue. She lifted her arm, keeping them above the waves. "Hold on tight," she warned them.

The water climbed over her chin and mouth, but she kept on going. *Do statues need to breathe?* Frankie wondered. Soon the sea swallowed her right up to her forehead. All that Frankie could see of her now were the tips of her crown. Then they disappeared too and the water rose up to her wrist.

"We're not going to make it," said Charlie. "We'll drown!"

But almost as soon as he had spoken, the water level began to drop. Gradually more and more of the statue emerged, dripping wet, as she marched out of the bay.

"Phew!" said Louise. "I knew she wouldn't let us down!"

Twenty metres or so from the shoreline, the statue stopped and reached out her hand to the harbour front. Frankie and the others hopped off.

"Thank you!" Ernie said, waving to the statue.

She smiled and let her hand slip back into the water.

Before any of the others could say anything, she began to walk back towards the island. Frankie watched her with a thumping heart. *I wish I'd had time to say thank you.*

"So how do we get to the stadium?" asked Louise, interrupting his thoughts. "You said we'd need a cab, right?"

"Do any of you have any money?" said Ernie.

Frankie shook his head. They never brought money on their adventures! "No. Have you?"

Ernie's face fell. "No, I don't. Which could be a problem," he said.

Frankie felt something tingle in his pocket, and he rummaged inside, pulling out a piece of paper.

"What's that?" asked Louise.

Frankie opened the paper. It was a one-dollar bill. There was a picture of a pyramid and an eagle on one side. Frankie turned it over. The reverse showed a man in a wig.

"Who's that?" asked Frankie.

"It's George Washington," said Louise. "The first President of the USA."

Ernie looked over his shoulder. "One buck won't even get us a block from here," he said. "The Yankee Stadium is on 161st, way north."

Frankie looked at the dollar bill in his hand. The face of the man on the note was oddly alive, with mischievous eyes, almost as if it was watching him.

"Why has this appeared in my pocket? It's completely useless," he muttered.

"Can we get a hot dog for a dollar?" asked Max hopefully.

*We can't just give up*, Frankie thought, raising his hand to flag a taxi. The traffic opened up, and a single yellow taxi came along the street. This car seemed bigger and brighter than the others, and the number plate read "AM DREAM". The taxi skidded to a halt beside Frankie and his friends, and the doors popped open.

"Did one of you good gentlemen and ladies summon transport?" came a voice from inside.

Frankie looked into the cab. The driver was an old man, with a thin face and rosy cheeks. He was wearing a red checked shirt and a yellow baseball cap. But sticking out from underneath the cap was what looked like an old-fashioned, curled wig, and his face was familiar . . . Frankie looked down at the dollar bill again, then back at the driver.

"Is it just me, or does he really look like George Washington?" Frankie asked.

"That's because I *am* George Washington," said the man. "Now hop in. And put that football in the trunk!"

# CHAPTER 4

They all climbed in. Frankie put the
football in the boot, then climbed
into the passenger seat. Max sat
on Charlie's knee in the back,
squeezed between Ernie and
Louise.

"Where to, my good fellow?"
asked George Washington.

"The Yankee Stadium," said Frankie.

Their driver started the engine, and the car growled into life. "Buckle up," he said.

Frankie hurriedly fastened his seatbelt, just as they shot off into the road. Cars swerved out of their way, beeping wildly.

"Slow down!" said Louise. "We'd like to get there in one piece!"

George Washington didn't seem to hear. He yanked on the steering wheel, skidding around a corner, his wig slipping on his head.

Frankie saw street signs flashing past. They'd only reached 4th

Street and it was 6.30pm according to the clock on the dashboard.

"How long until the try-out finishes?" he asked Ernie.

"Thirty minutes," replied his new friend. Ernie's face looked worried.

"Better step on it, then," said George Washington. He jammed his foot on the pedal and the car went even faster.

The taxi bounced around a corner on to a road called 5th Avenue. Posh-looking clothes shops lined the streets. Frankie saw one building rising above all the others, its summit a spike hundreds of metres up.

"Is that the Empire State Building?" he asked.

"Yeah," said Ernie. "You can go right to the top in a lift. The view from up there is amazing!"

"Would you like to take a look?" asked George Washington.

"Not now," said Frankie. "We have to get to the Yankee Stadium, remember?"

"Oh, don't be a killjoy," said Washington. He steered down another street, scattering pedestrians. Frankie heard the wail of a police siren behind him.

"Great," said Louise. "The cops!"

Looking in the mirror, Frankie

saw two police cars on their tail. "Better pull over," he said.

"Nonsense," said George Washington. He pushed a button on the dashboard, and the nose of the car lifted. Frankie's stomach dropped as the street fell away beneath them and the cab climbed into the air. He fell back in his seat, his body tense. They were careering right towards the side of the Empire State Building!

"We're going to crash!" barked Max.

Frankie glanced over and saw that George Washington had his eyes squeezed shut.

The car's bonnet rose, until they were travelling straight up the side of the building. Windows flashed past. Craning to look back, Frankie saw the police cars far below. His heart was somewhere in his throat.

"These automobiles are fantastic, aren't they?" said George Washington. Frankie saw he had his hands off the wheels and was leafing through a guide book. His bushy eyebrows shot up. "Apparently the Empire State Building is a hundred and three storeys tall! Imagine taking the stairs!"

This taxi had to be magic. There

was no way someone could drive a flying car and read at the same time. Frankie felt his body start to relax. He'd been in a flying sleigh and on a flying dragon before. This journey through the air had to be down to the magic football. He could hear it bouncing about in the boot of the cab!

They soared past the top floor, where Frankie spied tourists looking out from a viewing platform. The cab levelled off, and the city spun below.

Washington put his hands back on the wheel and steered across the sky. Frankie twisted round in his seat. In the back seat, his friends were gaping out of the windows.

"That's the Hudson River!" said Ernie, pointing to a silvery snake of water. Suddenly, the car juddered and dropped in the air. They all cried out. Smoke was belching from the exhaust.

"Oh dear," said George Washington.

The car started moving in fits and starts, throwing them around in their seats. Maybe the football's magic wasn't so strong, after all.

The nose of the car slowly dipped and Frankie's stomach did a somersault of terror.

"We need to lose some weight!" said Washington. "What about the dog?"

"Oh, thank you *very* much!" said Max.

Frankie spotted some green space up ahead. It looked massive — several blocks across and at least a mile long. "What about landing there?" he said, pointing. The grass looked nice and soft.

"That's Central Park!" said Ernie. "Can we make it?"

They were still higher than most of the buildings, but the cab's engine was sputtering dangerously.

"With a bit of good fortune, we may," said Washington. He steered the cab towards the park. "Ooh — there's Times Square!" he added, pointing out of the window.

Frankie saw huge flashing billboards, but couldn't get excited. They were losing height fast. The cars beneath looked bigger by the second, and buildings flashed past on either side. The park was still three blocks away. How were they going to land safely?

They were a hundred feet up.

Then fifty.

"Hold on tight!" said Washington.

The taxi fell with a sickening lurch. The ground was speeding towards them, and Frankie squeezed his eyes tight shut.

# CHAPTER 5

Frankie expected to hear the
horrible sound of metal colliding
with metal, but instead the wheels
thudded into the ground. He
opened his eyes and saw that they
were careering over grass, straight
for a tree. Frankie reached over
and swung the wheel round. They

missed the tree trunk by a hair's breadth. The cab bounced over the grass, then over a path, before shooting down a slope. George Washington was stamping his foot on a pedal.

"No brakes!" he cried. More trees loomed ahead.

"Hang on, everyone!" he said, yanking the wheel.

The cab skidded sideways, towards a pond, then flipped right around. With a crunch, the car's rear end slumped into the water. They had stopped.

Everyone sat in silence. Frankie's heart was thudding so fast he could barely feel the individual beats.

"Are you all okay?" he asked.

His friends nodded.

Frankie cracked open the door and climbed out. Smoke was billowing from under the bonnet. A few people had gathered around, some out walking their dogs, some in running kit. A couple of tourists were being carried around in a horse and cart.

"Woah! They must be filming a movie," someone said, pointing at Frankie and the others.

The man leading the horse and cart jumped down and rushed over.

"That was some crash!" he said. "Hey, where's the driver?"

Frankie pointed towards the cab's front seat. "He's right th—Oh!"

George Washington had disappeared.

"He's split!" said someone. "What a crook!"

Louise and Ernie got out of the cab, and Charlie carried Max.

Frankie went to the boot, and retrieved his magic football.

"Soccer fan, I see," said the horse and cart owner.

The cab's engine gave a couple of choking noises, and Frankie stepped back. "I'm not sure it's safe," said Louise. "Maybe we should get—"

The engine gave a loud bang, startling the horses. They whinnied in panic, reared up, then bolted off through the park, carrying the couple in the cart with them.

"Hey, stop!" cried the owner.

Frankie sprinted after the horses, magic football in hand. Louise and Charlie were running too, and Max was at Frankie's heels.

"Spread out!" he said.

The cart jolted up and down as the horses galloped away with the passengers screaming. The horses veered sideways towards some railings. They had to be stopped! Charlie hurled himself into their path, spreading his arms as if waiting for a penalty.

"Woah!" he cried. "Calm down!"

Frankie worried that his friend would be trampled, but the horses shied and started charging towards a set of open gates. On the other side was the road, with cars zooming past. *They'll be injured!* Frankie thought. He put on a burst of speed to stop the runaway cart. He counted under his breath. *One, two, three* . . . He drew level with the cart and leapt up into the driver's seat. He grabbed the reins and heaved back. The horses reared, hooves lashing the air. Louise had run round to stand in front of the horses. She walked slowly and carefully towards them.

"It's okay," she whispered. "Don't be scared."

Frankie knew that Louise was

good with horses, but she could easily get hurt. As she edged closer, the animals seemed to calm a little. Their nostrils still flared but they'd stopped kicking. The two passengers scrambled out of the cart and raced off, leaving Frankie alone in the driver's seat. As Frankie held his breath, Louise came closer and slowly reached out for the bridles, tugging the horses' heads down so that she could stroke their noses. They nudged her shoulders and blew warm breath into her face. Louise grinned up at Frankie.

"You did it," he gasped.

Louise shrugged. "It's just a

talent I have," she said, pretending it was nothing. But Frankie could see how proud she looked.

"If you ever stop playing football, you can take up horse training," he told her.

Louise's eyes widened in shock. "I'll never give up football!" They both laughed.

The owner arrived, breathing heavily.

"I can't thank you kids enough," he said. "What can I do to repay you?"

A sudden thought occurred to Frankie.

"You could give us a ride," he said.

"Sure!" said the man. "Where to?"

Frankie grinned, as Ernie came to arrive by his side. He put an arm around his friend's shoulders. "The Yankee Stadium."

"Ah, the Field of Dreams!" said the cart driver.

Frankie frowned. "Pardon?"

"That's what they call the baseball field," he said. "Sure, I'll take you."

# CHAPTER 6

The horses' hooves clattered across the tarmac. Frankie caught Ernie looking at his watch nervously. It was ten to seven — only a few minutes before the try-out session ended.

As they crossed a junction, Frankie saw the stadium for the

first time, rising high over the other buildings. "It looks just like a football ground from the outside," he said.

"It *is* a soccer ground sometimes!" said Ernie. "New York FC play here."

"I guess this is your stop," said the cart driver. "Good luck!"

Ernie thanked him and they hopped off. "Only five minutes left," said Frankie. "We'd better run."

They sprinted across a car park to the gates, where a bulky security guard was munching on something. Max's nose twitched. "Unless I'm mistaken," Frankie's dog said, "that is a real New York hot dog."

Ernie rushed up to the guard. "I'm here for the try-outs."

The guard grunted. "That right? Let's see your pass."

Ernie's face fell. "It's at home . . . "

"No pass, no entry," said the guard, taking another bite of his hot dog.

Louise touched Frankie's shoulder lightly. "Come on Frankie – let's not cause trouble."

*She's got a plan,* Frankie thought, allowing himself to be led away with the others.

"And no ball games in the car park either," the guard shouted after them.

When they were out of sight further around the stadium wall, Louise talked quickly.

"How accurate are you with that ball, Frankie?" she asked.

"Pretty accurate," he said.

"Good," said Louise. "Now listen up."

She outlined her plan, and Frankie got his football ready. If he missed, the scheme would fail completely *and* they'd end up in all sorts of trouble.

Creeping back around so the

guard was in sight, Frankie looked at Max. "Ready, boy?"

"Ready and hungry," said Max.

Frankie placed the ball on the ground, aimed, and fired with his right foot. The ball curled through the air, and clipped the guard's hat right off his head.

"Hey! What?" he exclaimed. He bent to retrieve it. As he did, Max shot out. With a leap, he clamped his teeth over the hot dog and scampered away.

"Little mutt!" yelled the guard, giving chase.

"Now's our chance," said Louise. They all ran from their hiding place

and slipped through the gate into the stadium. Frankie picked up his ball as he passed.

"Follow me!" said Ernie, leading the way.

The inside of the stadium was a maze. All the food and gift stalls were closed for the night. It was eerily quiet. They followed signs for the stands, and soon they reached a tunnel. Coming the other way were lots of young kids in sports gear with their parents.

"Do you think I'll get in?" said a girl.

"I don't know, sweetheart," said her mum. "But you did your best — that's what counts."

"We're too late!" cried Ernie.

"I'm not giving up that easily," Frankie muttered. "Come on!"

The tunnel emerged on to a pitch of green grass, lined with soaring stands of empty seats. Frankie's heart did a flip — he loved stadiums.

The air was alive with a sense of history and excitement. Giant floodlights lit up the pitch as a team of men in all white strips warmed up by running sprints. A couple were wearing helmets and swinging bats, and others were hurling a baseball between each other and making catches. One man was much older, with grey hair peeping out from under a baseball cap. His jacket read "COACH."

Ernie ran right up to him. "Hello, sir!" he said. "My name's Ernie Tanner. I'm here for the try-out." He swelled his chest. "I want to be a pitcher."

The coach glanced down at Ernie. "Then you're an hour too late. The try-out's over. It's Senior Team practice now."

He turned back to the other players.

"Please let me give it a shot," said Ernie.

The coach shook his head. "Kid, playing for this team is about more than being able to pitch a ball. It's about respect, too. You can't just show up late."

Frankie ran to Ernie's side. "It wasn't his fault," he said desperately.

The coach rolled his eyes. "It never is!" he said. He pointed to a couple of the senior players. "All right, fellas, let's get started . . . "

"No!" said Frankie angrily. The coach looked at him, glowering. Frankie realised this was his last chance to help Ernie. "Ernie never thought he'd even make it here tonight," he said." He's gone through a lot. You can't just turn around and tell him his dream's worth nothing."

Another player, carrying a bat, came up behind him. "Maybe cut him some slack, boss," he said. "You never know, he might be the next big thing. Don't want him going to the Mets, huh?"

Ernie leaned closer to Frankie. "That's the other New York baseball team," he said.

Frankie held his breath. The coach's eyes softened a little. "Tell you what, Ernie," he said. "I'll give you a chance."

The coach tapped his batter on the back. "If you can get Horatio here out, you'll get an automatic spot on the juniors. How about it?"

Ernie swallowed. "Him?"

The batter grinned. "There's your shot, kid. Don't waste it."

"He won't," said Frankie.

"All right, then," said the coach. "Get yourselves lined up."

The batter nodded and ran back towards the batting plate. Ernie was trembling. "Horatio Chappelle is a professional baseball player. He's a *superstar*! He'll hit me out of the park." He looked at his feet. "Thank you for all your help, but . . . I can't do it!"

# CHAPTER 7

Frankie looked at Ernie. He had to do something! He thought of all the times he'd been scared, too. Scared of missing a penalty, scared of losing. He remembered what his coach had told him.

"You were good enough to get

a try-out, weren't you?" he said to
Ernie.

"I guess so," said Ernie.

"You've got to believe in
yourself," added Louise.

"Grab your dream," said Charlie.
"We believe in you."

Ernie set his mouth in a grim line
of determination. "You're right.
Thanks, guys!"

"You three other kids might as
well get in the outfield," the coach
called over.

Frankie and Louise ran across
the turf. Frankie could only imagine
what this place would be like filled
with screaming fans. The noise

would be deafening. Charlie stayed back and tapped the coach on the shoulder. "Hey, could I be the catcher?" he asked with a cheeky smile. "It's kind of my speciality."

The coach laughed. "Sure, kid. You've got to be sharp though — those balls come pretty fast."

"I'm *always* sharp," said Charlie. He found a mitt on the ground and put it on, then took up position behind the batting plate.

Ernie walked slowly towards the pitcher's spot, and one of the other players tossed him a ball. He caught it, then stood facing Horatio.

"Whenever you're ready," said

the batter. "Good luck, Ernie – I'm not going to make it easy for you."

"You can do it!" shouted Frankie.

He saw Ernie suck in a deep breath as he turned side-on, keeping the ball hidden behind his leading arm. Then he spun, his arm lashing like a whip. A split-second later, Charlie was on his back on the ground. Frankie didn't even know what had happened until Charlie lifted the mitt and he saw the ball inside.

"Strike one!" shouted the coach. Frankie glanced at Louise, who looked as amazed as he felt. "He's *fast!*" she said.

Charlie tossed the ball back to
Ernie, who waved to Frankie.

The blood had rushed to
Horatio's face. "Beginner's luck," he
said. "You won't be able to do that
again."

Frankie saw Ernie adjust his grip
a fraction on the ball. He didn't look
scared any more.

*Go on!* urged Frankie. *Show him
how much this means to you* . . .

Ernie's second pitch left his hand
too early, and the ball looked to be
heading wide, but then it curled
in mid-air, swinging inwards.
Horatio had to shift his feet as he
swung and the ball shot beneath his

bat, right into Charlie's glove.

"Strike two!" yelled the coach. "You're being beaten by a kid, Horatio," he said.

Horatio glared at Ernie. "No more playing around," he said.

Ernie had the ball again. He tossed it from hand to hand.

"One more and you're in the junior team," said the coach.

"No chance!" Horatio muttered.

Ernie spun again, hurling the ball hard and straight. But it was just at the right height and the baseball bat met it perfectly. Frankie saw the small white ball climb in a high looping arc. Ernie twisted and watched it sail over his head, his face a picture of dismay.

Frankie began running. He heard Louise cry, "Catch it, Frankie!" as he sprinted beneath the ball's flight. He didn't know if he would make it, but he had to try. He pushed his legs to run faster, as if he were chasing a long pass over the top for a match-winning goal. The floodlights dazzled him as he kept his eyes fixed on the ball. It reached the top of its flight and began to fall. Nothing mattered but getting there in time. It fell fast, and Frankie's feet slipped on

the turf. When he was about six
metres from the falling baseball
he threw himself through the air,
right arm outstretched, fingers

into his palm
n slammed
to his side.

He struggled to breathe, winded.

"He's out!" he heard the coach cry.

Through the grass, Frankie saw Charlie running towards Ernie and leaping on top of him with a whoop. Louise reached Frankie's side.

"Super catch!" she said, helping him to his feet. "We did it! Ernie's on the team."

"I don't know how to thank you guys enough," said Ernie.

They were standing at the side of the pitch five minutes later, watching the senior team practise. Horatio was still being mocked by his team-mates.

"Maybe you should join the junior team," one said.

Frankie looked at Ernie's beaming face. "Just make sure you always believe in yourself," he said. "Live your dream."

"I will!" said Ernie. He shook his head. "All of today feels like a dream. It's been crazy. That soccer ball of yours is something special."

Frankie clutched the magic football under his arm. "It gets us into some fun adventures," he said.

They heard the scuffle of paws, and Max came trotting down the tunnel. He had the remains of a hot dog in his mouth, and dropped it at his feet.

"I think . . . we had . . . better get out of . . . here," he panted.

"Why?" said Frankie.

"Someone catch that dog!" yelled an angry voice. The security guard came barrelling down the tunnel.

Max swallowed the rest of the hot dog in one mouthful.

"I know another way out!" said Ernie. "Follow me!"

He led them around the edge of the field to another tunnel. It was very dark inside, and Frankie could barely see Ernie's shape ahead of him, but he could hear the footsteps of his friends at his heels.

"Hey, wait!" he called out.

Ernie didn't reply, then Frankie
felt the ground disappear beneath
his feet. He reached out to break
his fall, but the impact never came.
His body went spinning down, into
some dark abyss. Then, with a jolt,
he found himself standing on grass
again, blinking into bright light. He
saw trees, and a goal, and a park
beyond. *The* park. Back home.

Charlie was sitting on the goal–
line, with Max sniffing at the glove
on his hand. Louise was looking
about herself. Frankie was holding
the magic football.

"I'm guessing that wasn't a dream," he said.

Charlie stood up. "I don't think so," he said. "Max has got mustard on his whiskers."

Frankie's dog licked his chops.

Louise laughed. "I wonder what happened to Ernie. I hope he got magicked back to the Statue of Liberty!"

Frankie looked at the football in his hands. "I'm sure the football's magic will keep him safe. It made his dream come true, after all."

"With a little help from us," said Louise. "Anyway, the try-out is just the start. Ernie will have to work hard to make it to the Major League."

Frankie remembered the determination on Ernie's face as he'd stood on the pitcher's spot. "I reckon he's got what it takes," he said. "One day, he might be as famous as Joe DiMaggio!"

Charlie was staring at the glove on his hand. "You know what," he said. "I *really* like baseball."

Frankie nodded. "Yeah, but not as much as football."

"Of course not," said Charlie. "Nothing beats football!"

# ACKNOWLEDGEMENTS

Many thanks to everyone at Little, Brown Book Group; Neil Blair, Zoe King, Daniel Teweles and all at The Blair Partnership; Luella Wright for bringing my characters to life; special thanks to Michael Ford for all his wisdom and patience;